The Detective Club:
Buried Treasure!

'The Detective Club: Buried Treasure!'
An original concept by Elizabeth Dale
© Elizabeth Dale

Illustrated by Kelly O'Neill

Published by MAVERICK ARTS PUBLISHING LTD
Studio 3A, City Business Centre, 6 Brighton Road,
Horsham, West Sussex, RH13 5BB
© Maverick Arts Publishing Limited March 2019
+44 (0)1403 256941

A CIP catalogue record for this book is available at the British Library.

ISBN 978-1-84886-435-1

Maverick
publishing
www.maverickbooks.co.uk

White

This book is rated as: White Band (Guided Reading)

The Detective Club:
Buried Treasure!

By **Elizabeth Dale**

Illustrated by
Kelly O'Neill

Chapter 1

"No way!"

Fiz, Amir and Leo gasped as they stared into the hole they'd just dug. For there, at the bottom, was a big chest.

"I told you!" Fiz cried, holding her spade high and twirling around in glee.

Leo and Amir laughed. Fiz's real name was Fiona, but everyone called her Fiz. She was

always fizzing with excitement, like a shaken
bottle of lemonade!

"But that's just an old chest, Fiz – it's nothing
like what we're looking for!" said Leo.

A local bank had recently been burgled, and the
three friends had decided to hunt for the stolen
gold bars.

"The gold is probably inside the chest!"
Fiz cried. "Didn't I say someone's been digging
here? You thought it was badgers – but look
what we found! Woo-hoo! The Detective Club
solves its first crime! Come on, help me
open it!"

They tugged and tugged, and finally managed to lift the lid.

"Oh!" cried everyone.

"That's not gold bars from the robbery," said Amir.

It wasn't. All they could see were small, dark discs.

"They look old," said Fiz, pulling some out.

"Very old!" sighed Amir. "I think this chest has been here a long time. Shame!"

"Not necessarily!" cried Leo, his eyes shining. "I reckon we've found Roman treasure!"

Chapter 2

The friends grabbed a handful of discs each.
Then they covered the hole with leaves and soil,
and hurried round to the local museum.

"These are very interesting coins," said Mr
Jones, the curator, peering at them.

"Are they Roman?" asked Leo eagerly.

"No," he said, and everyone groaned. "But I
think they're Saxon – and very valuable!

Wait there!"

Fiz, Leo and Amir were stunned. They'd found Saxon treasure!

Mr Jones hurried back in with a woman dressed in a white coat. "This is Professor Mixom, the county's Saxon expert," he said. "She'll confirm it for sure."

Professor Mixom smiled at the children.

"Show me the coins!" she said. And then her face fell.

"These aren't Saxon!" she cried, poking them with her long, red nails. "They're fake coins, probably props used in a film."

"Are you sure?" Mr Jones frowned. "Shouldn't we send them to be checked over?"

"No!" said Professor Mixom sharply. "I'm the Saxon expert, remember?"

The children sadly watched as Mr Jones put the coins in a drawer. As they walked away, Professor Mixom caught up with them.

"Where did you find the coins?" she asked.

"Buried in a chest in Windmill Field," said Leo.

"On the right, just past the gate," added Amir. "We covered it back over with leaves."

"Good! Look, you must leave it alone now and don't tell anyone," said the professor. "We don't want anybody finding it and pretending they're Saxon coins."

Fiz, Leo and Amir frowned. Really?! They'd been so excited to find treasure. But not only was it all fake, they couldn't even tell anyone about it.

The next morning Fiz rushed round to Amir's house. Leo was there – having a second breakfast.

"I've lost my favourite bracelet," she told them. "I think it might've fallen off when we were digging yesterday. Can you help me find it?"

"Okay!" said Leo, grabbing his third piece of toast while Amir picked up his detecting bag full of useful crime-solving gadgets.

Amir found the bracelet lying in the grass near the hole.

"Great!" Fiz smiled. "Thanks, Amir!"

Then they all gazed sadly at the hole, covered over as they'd left it. Or was it? Leo frowned. The leaves didn't seem to fill it completely. Suddenly he jumped into the hole – and sank deep into the leaves.

"Just as I thought!" he cried. "The hole's empty apart from the leaves. The chest's been stolen!"

Chapter 3

The children ran straight back to the museum and told Mr Jones.

"We have to tell Professor Mixom!" Leo cried.

"She's in her office," said Mr Jones. "I'll take you."

Professor Mixom was very cross to hear the news.

"What?!" she cried. "I told you not to tell anyone about the chest." And she pointed at the children angrily with one chipped red nail.

"We didn't!" Fiz cried.

"Strangely, the coins you kids found have disappeared from my drawer too," Mr Jones said.

"How odd," said the professor. "I'll have to notify museums to be wary of fake Saxon treasure. I've got a meeting now, I'll deal with this later."

As they walked back down the corridor, Fiz whispered to the others. "Professor Mixom's nails... did you notice them?"

"No," said Amir.

"They were chipped. And yet yesterday they were so perfect..."

Leo stopped. "It was her! She knew where the chest was. She chipped her nails when she dug it up."

"But she said it wasn't worth very much!" Amir whispered.

"But Mr Jones thought it was!" Leo said. "I think she lied to us! She told us to keep away from it so we wouldn't know she'd taken it!"

"Let's hide here," said Fiz, suddenly darting behind a display cabinet.

"What are you doing?" Amir hissed.

"Professor Mixom said she was going to a meeting," Fiz said. "As soon as she leaves, we can nip in and search her office."

"We can't! What if she comes back and catches us in there?" Amir asked.

Leo sighed. "Sometimes, Amir, you just have to be brave!"

Chapter 4

Suddenly Professor Mixom's door opened and everyone ducked down. They heard her shut it and then the click of a key turning.

"No! She's locked the door!" Leo whispered as she hurried away.

Once the professor was out of sight, Fiz jumped up. "Quick!" she cried, racing in the other direction.

"There must be spare keys," Fiz continued.
"We'll just have to think of an excuse to ask Mr
Jones for them – or maybe we can creep into his
office and find them."

But Amir didn't want any part in stealing keys
or secretly searching offices. Instead he
decided to follow the professor and listen
outside her meeting. Maybe he'd overhear
something useful...?

But as he turned the corner he saw that the
fire-escape door was open and the professor
was rushing across the car park!

Amir nipped outside too and darted down
behind a car. Professor Mixom had her back to

him and was unlocking her boot.

He gasped as he saw her take a clear plastic bag out of her pocket. It was full of coins. Their coins! She'd stolen them from Mr Jones' drawer! And then she lifted the boot to reveal their chest. So she'd stolen that, too!

As Amir watched, Professor Mixom tipped the coins into the chest, then closed the boot and climbed into her driving seat.

No! She was going to get away with all the treasure. Amir panicked. What could he do? Leo and Fiz would know. They'd stop her somehow. If only he was brave like them!

Chapter 5

Suddenly, the professor climbed out of her car. She was talking on her mobile phone.

Amir ducked down quickly, pulled out the mini-recorder from his detecting bag and switched it on.

"I'll just nip back and get it from the office," she said, walking past the car Amir was hiding behind. She quickly glanced over her shoulder to check nobody could hear, and added, "yes, the chest is full of Saxon treasure, there are goblets and jewels under the coins! We're going to make a fortune when we sell it all in America."

Amir was stunned. The chest was full of treasure that she was going to sell! He hurried inside after the professor. Her office door was open, with her keys still in the lock.

Quick as a flash, Amir shut the door. His fingers trembled as he locked it. At once, the professor started hammering on the door, yelling, "Let me out!"

Amir raced to the exhibition rooms where Leo and Fiz were talking to Mr Jones.

"What's that noise?" asked Mr Jones.

"It's Professor Mixom!" panted Amir. "I've locked her in her office!" And he held up the keys.

"Amir!" cried Leo.

"Let her out immediately!" thundered Mr Jones.

Amir faltered. "But she's got the treasure chest and our stolen coins in her car. I overheard her telling someone they're worth a fortune."

"I don't believe it," said Mr Jones, holding out his hand. "Give me those keys."

"But… but she's planning to sell it all in America. I recorded her conversation here!" Amir cried, holding up the mini-recorder. "Listen!"

Everyone gasped as he re-played the professor's confession. This proved everything!

"Look, her car keys are on her office key ring!" Amir said, grinning. "Come and see what she's stolen!"

Everyone rushed out to the car and saw for themselves that the treasure chest was most definitely there, and it was huge! Mr Jones couldn't believe his eyes as he gazed at the coins, goblets and jewels.

"Incredible!" he gasped.

"Well done, Amir!" Leo cried. "You found the treasure and the stolen coins."

"And you've proved the professor was stealing them! All on your own!" Fiz said. "You're a hero!"

And as Mr Jones rang the police, Amir smiled happily.

The Detective Club had solved their first crime! And he was a hero! Amazing!

The End

Book Bands for Guided Reading

The Institute of Education book banding system is a scale of colours that reflects the various levels of reading difficulty. The bands are assigned by taking into account the content, the language style, the layout and phonics. Word, phrase and sentence level work is also taken into consideration.

Maverick Early Readers are a bright, attractive range of books covering the pink to white bands. All of these books have been book banded for guided reading to the industry standard and edited by a leading educational consultant.

Pink
Red
Yellow
Blue
Green
Orange
Turquoise
Purple
Gold
White

To view the whole Maverick Readers scheme, visit our website at
www.maverickearlyreaders.com

Or scan the QR code above to view our scheme instantly!